For Paddy, Tom, Jack, and Leon.

First published in 2004 by The Bear Shop Book Co.,
an imprint of Emma Treehouse Ltd.,
Old Brewhouse, Shepton Mallet BA4 5QE
Text and illustrations copyright © 2004 by Rikey Austin
All rights reserved
ISBN 1 85576 414 8
Printed in China
2 4 6 8 10 9 7 5 3 1

Cobby

Goes for a Swim

Rikey Austin

The Bear Shop Book Co.

Cobby and his boy were on a boat trip. The boy, whose name was Tom, was having a wonderful time watching a pair of dolphins who had come to play around the boat. But Cobby was not enjoying himself. He was too small to see over the side of the boat.

He waved his arms, hoping to be noticed, but he wasn't.

He jumped up and down, but still nobody noticed.

He climbed up to the rail and peered excitedly over

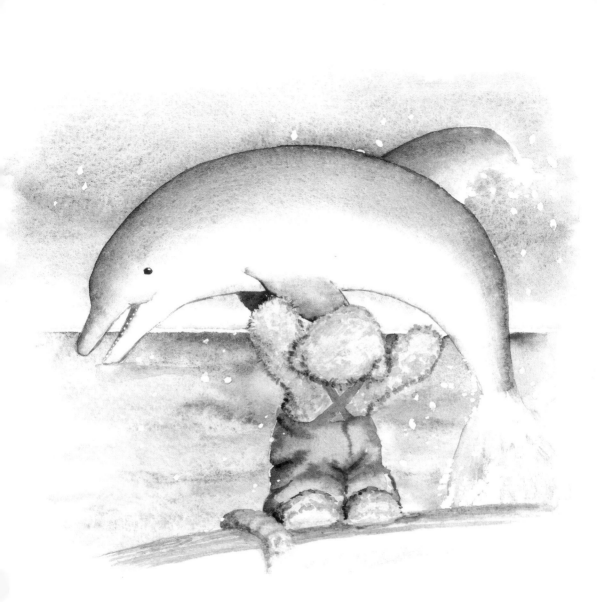

to see a dolphin leap into the air right
in front of him, showering everybody with
gemlike drops of seawater. Cobby clapped his
hands in joy. What an adventure!

Cobby fell,

head over heels.

Splash!

The first thing he saw when he came
spluttering to the surface was a big orange
buoy. Cobby paddled toward it and clung
to it tightly. Luckily the sea was calm.
"Now what?" he thought.

Then he said
to himself:
"I'll shout."

But the boat was sailing away, and no one could hear him calling. He was, after all, a little bear with a very little voice.

A seagull landed on the buoy and pecked at him to see if he was good to eat, and then flew away again.

He was sure there were little fishes nibbling on his toes.

Then he heard a noise behind him.

"Now what?"
he was thinking again,
as he turned around.
What he saw surprised him so much
he almost let go of the buoy.

It was the dolphin swimming alongside a pretty little rowboat.

"Well, what do we have here?" chuckled the man at the oars. "The world-famous lobster-pot thief?" And he laughed gently.

Cobby sighed. He was not in the mood
for jokes, and he was very tired of his
adventure by now. His paws were cold, he
was covered with seaweed, and he had a nasty
feeling that he had torn a hole in his favorite
overalls.

The fisherman leaned over and picked him up by the ear.

"Goodness! You weigh a ton," said the man as he dumped him in the bottom of the boat. Cobby was not surprised. He had felt the cold seawater soaking slowly into his stuffing for some time.

A crab in a lobster pot in the bottom of the boat nipped at him. Cobby sighed deeply and his chin began to wobble. The fisherman leaned down and patted him gently with one rough brown hand.

"It's OK, little bear. I know just the people to take care of you," he said as he lifted him up onto a seat.

The fisherman pulled in the rest of
his pots, then rowed steadily back toward
the land.

The fisherman took the dripping bear to
Alice's Bear Shop, which is just a stone's throw
from the beach. Alice and her mom were
famous in the town. Children (and grown-ups)
from miles around brought sick and hurt bears
to Alice's Bear Shop, knowing
that Alice could make
them better.

Alice immediately made a sign to put in the window while her mom filled a bowl with warm soapy water. This is what the sign said:

Found.
Bear lost at sea.
Soggy but safe.

Inquire within.

Alice washed his overalls and found a patch for the knee, while the little bear was put on the radiator to dry.

Some time later Alice felt his paws to see how dry he was and lifted him down.

"Don't be sad," said Alice. "You're a lovely bear and I'm sure that your boy will come soon."

Cobby shook his head sadly. "He'll never think of looking here, and I have had such a terrible adventure."

"Nonsense. Everybody knows that this is where lost bears come," said Alice kindly.

She hugged him while he wiped a tear from his cheek. "Why don't you tell me what happened?"

The little bear began, jumping around and acting out his part. In his story the sea was stormy, the gull became an eagle, the fishes sharks, and the kindly fisherman a pirate, but the funny thing was that as he told his story he began to giggle,

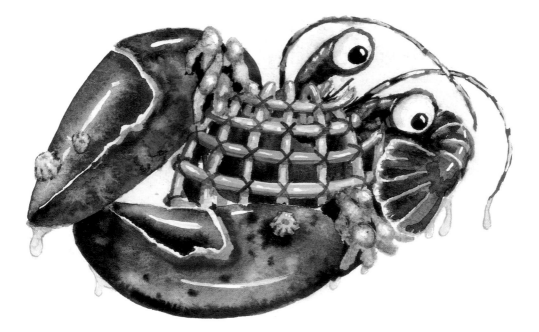

and by the time he told Alice about the
crab in the pot (which he described as a
monstrous lobster) she was hugging her
belly and rolling with laughter.

The shop bell rang and in came a
worried-looking boy. It was Cobby's boy.
He saw Cobby right away and his face
lit up.

"Cobby. You're here! I thought I'd lost
you forever." Tom hugged his bear close.
Cobby was definitely a loved-to-bits bear.

Before they left Alice's Bear Shop, Alice handed Tom a backpack.

"You can carry him in this," she said. "A curious bear like that can get into all kinds of trouble if he can't see what's going on!"